Happy Cat First Readers

The Magic Wand

Becky just wants her annoying
little brother to disappear.
Then, with a wave of her magic
wand, he does just that and
Becky tries every trick in the
book to get him back...

D0332661

Happy Cat First Readers

The Magic Wand

Ursula
Dubosarsky

Illustrated by
Mitch Vane

HAPPY CAT BOOKS

Published by
Happy Cat Books
An imprint of Catnip Publishing Ltd
Islington Business Centre
3-5 Islington High Street
London N1 9LQ

First published by Penguin Books, Australia, 2002

This edition first published 2006
1 3 5 7 9 10 8 6 4 2

A CIP catalogue record for this book is available
from the British Library

ISBN 10: 1 905117 24 8
ISBN 13: 978-1-905117-24-6

Printed in Poland

www.catnippublishing.co.uk

For Debbie Johnston,

with much love from us all. *U.D.*

For my beautiful Talia and

her loving brother Jordie. *M.V.*

Chapter One

One day, when everything
was very quiet, Becky
found a long thin stick
under a pile of leaves
in the back garden.

She bent down and
picked it up.

It was an old paintbrush.

All its hair had fallen out.

It was covered with dirt.

'It's just the right size,'

thought Becky.

Chapter Two

She took the stick over to the hose and washed it. Her feet got wet. So did her shirt when she dried the stick on it.

Then she went inside into the kitchen, and opened up the drawer with all the

knives and forks.

Squashed right up the
back was a long piece
of ribbon left over from
a birthday present.

She pulled it out. It was
purple and gold and shiny.
She wound the ribbon
round and round the stick,
wrapping it tight. She stuck

some old chewing gum at each end, so the ribbon wouldn't fall off.

Then she stood in the middle of the room and waved it about in the air.

'Abracadabra!' said Becky.

Chapter Three

Becky's little brother came into the kitchen.

He couldn't talk much, but he could look. He looked at Becky.

'It's a magic wand,' said Becky, waving it at him. 'You'd better watch out.'

She went back out into
the back garden. Her little
brother came after her.

'Abracadabra!' said Becky,
pointing her wand at
a pebble.

'Abracadabra!' she said,
pointing it at a dead flower.

'Abracadabra!' she said,
pointing it at a snail.

Becky's little brother was
very impressed.

Chapter Four

Becky went further into the back garden. Her little brother came after her.

'Stop following me!' said Becky.

He didn't stop. He just kept coming.

Becky went even further

into the back garden.

'Go away!' she said.

'You're annoying me.'

But he didn't go away.

He kept on coming.

Becky went so far into
the back garden that she
reached the fence, and she
couldn't go any further.

'If you don't leave me alone,' she said to her little brother, 'I'll put a spell on you.'

He kept on coming.

Chapter Five

Becky was really cross now.

'It's your own fault,' she said to her little brother. 'I warned you.'

She lifted up her magic wand. She waved it round and round. Then she pointed it straight at him.

He looked scared.

She closed her eyes and shouted in her most terrible and mysterious voice:

'ABRACADABRA!!'

There was a silence.

She opened her eyes.

Her little brother was gone!

Chapter Six

Becky stepped down from the fence. She looked up and down and from side to side. He was all gone.

'Ed?' she said. 'Ed? Are you there?'

Becky went right into the middle of the garden. 'Ed?'

Her little brother was
nowhere.

'It worked!' thought
Becky, pleased. She patted

her magic wand. 'It really worked.'

Then she thought: 'I wonder where he's gone to?'

'Miaow,' said a black cat,
stepping out from behind
a bush.

Chapter Seven

The black cat came over
and sat down in front of
her. Becky had never seen
it before. Its long tail curled
in the air.

'Miaow,' said the black cat.

It couldn't talk, but it
could look.

It looked at Becky.

Becky stared into its big
yellow eyes.

It couldn't be – could it?
The black cat rolled over
and stretched out its claws.

Could it?

'Is that you, Ed?' said

Becky.

Chapter Eight

'Miaow,' said the black cat. 'Miaow, miaow.'

It came up very close.

'It is you, isn't it, Ed?' said Becky.

'Miaow,' said the cat again. 'Miaow, miaow, miaow, miaow.'

Becky put her hands over her ears.

'Be quiet, for a moment, will you?' she said.

The cat was quiet.

Becky took her hands off her ears.

'Miaow,' said the black cat.

Becky walked away, right up to the end of the garden. The cat followed her.

'Miaow, miaow, miaow.'

She walked quickly to

the other end of the garden.

The cat followed her.

'Go away!' said Becky.

'Miaow, miaow, miaow,

miaow, miaow, miaow,

miaow, miaow, miaow,

miaow, miaow, miaow!'

It was awful.

It was even worse than before she put the spell on him.

Chapter Nine

Becky ran as fast as she could down into the house. She slammed the back door so the cat couldn't get in.

'Oh, there you are, Becky,' said Becky's mother. 'Have you seen Ed?'

Becky hid the magic

wand behind her back.

'Um,' she said. 'He's
outside, I think.'

'Could you go and get
him?' said Becky's mother.

'I've just made a chocolate
cake.'

Becky's mother opened
the oven. Becky saw the
chocolate cake sitting there

in the pan, lovely and
plump and warm.

'I don't think he's hungry,'
she said, staring at the
cake.

'He's always hungry,' said
Becky's mother. 'Go and get
him, will you?'

'Oh, all right,' said Becky.

Chapter Ten

Becky went back outside. It was no good, she would have to change him back.

Becky's mother wouldn't be very happy if Ed came in for chocolate cake looking like a cat.

The cat was lying
stretched out under a tree.
'Don't open your mouth!'
said Becky. 'I'll change you
back, all right?'

The cat didn't say

anything. It looked at

Becky and blinked.

Becky raised the magic

wand in the air. She waved

it about in a circle. She

pointed it at the cat and

closed her eyes.

'Abracadabra!'

She opened her eyes.

'Miaow,' said the cat.

Becky frowned. She shook
the wand. She twirled it
in the air. She tried again.

'Abracadabra!'

But nothing changed.
There was the
cat. There
was no little
brother.

Chapter Eleven

Then, just as she was
about to try for the third
time, the cat sprang from
the ground. It bounded
up the trunk of the tree
and up into a high
branch.

'Just a minute, Ed!' said

Becky. 'I'm sure it will work

this time.'

The cat leapt from the

tree onto the fence.

'Wait!' said Becky in a panic.

The cat ran along the fence on its four black feet. Then . . .

'No! Come back!' cried
Becky.

But it was too late. The
cat jumped from the fence
into the neighbour's garden.

Becky ran over to the fence. It was very tall. She couldn't look over it, so she peered through the cracks in the wood.

All she could see were thick dark green leaves. It was like a jungle in there. The black cat had disappeared from sight.

Chapter Twelve

Becky sat down on the ground to think. What could she do next?

'Poor Ed,' she thought. 'What if a dog chases him?'

Becky thought a lot.

She thought about her magic wand. She thought

about the cat. She thought
about Ed. She thought
about her mother.

Then she thought about
the chocolate cake.

'It's no good,' she decided,
standing up, her hands on
her hips. 'I'm just going
to have to tell her.'

Chapter Thirteen

Becky walked down to the house, into the kitchen through the back door.

'Becky,' said her mother, 'where have you been?'

Becky opened her mouth to speak. She held out the magic wand.

'Mum,' she began. 'You
see –'

Then she noticed
something.

Something hiding behind her mother's legs. Something with chocolate crumbs smeared all over his face.

Something that looked
rather pleased with himself.
'Ed?' said Becky.

'You're just in time,' said Becky's mother. 'There's only one piece of cake left.'

Then she pointed at the magic wand that Becky was holding out.

'What's that?' she asked.

'Oh, nothing,' said Becky quickly, letting her hand fall. 'Just a stick.'

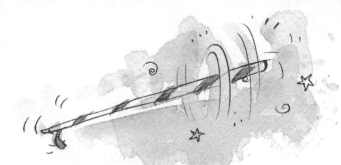

Chapter Fourteen

Becky's mother went into the living room to watch television. Becky ate the last piece of chocolate cake and drank a glass of very cold milk.

She looked at the magic wand. She wondered.

Should she take off the
ribbon and the chewing
gum, and put the stick back
under the pile of leaves
where she had found it?

She shook her head
slowly.

'I don't think I will,' said
Becky.

She got up and went over
to the drawer with all the
knives and forks. She put
the magic wand right at

the back, where nobody
could see.

Well, nearly nobody.

Her little brother was right

behind her, thumb in his mouth, watching.

'I'm going to get you one day for that,' hissed Becky, turning on him. 'Just you wait.'

Becky's little brother took his thumb out of his mouth. He couldn't talk much but he could look. He looked at Becky.

'Miaow,' said Becky's little brother.

From Ursula Dubosarsky

A long time ago I made myself a magic wand out of an old paintbrush that I covered all over with sticky black paint. I waved it around in the air and did lots and lots of magic spells. But, like Becky, I was never quite sure if they worked or not.

I didn't keep it but I wish I had. It might have come in handy one day!

From Mitch Vane

Becky and Ed are just like my own kids. My son Jordie adores his big sister and follows her everywhere. Talia is always telling him to leave her alone, but when he actually does go away, she gets bored and wants him back again.

Wouldn't we all like a magic wand like Becky's? As long as it worked when you wanted it to!

The Princess and the Unicorn

Wendy Blaxland

No one believes in unicorns any more. Except Princess Lily, that is.
So when the king falls ill and the only thing that can cure him is
the magic of a unicorn, it's up to her to find one.
But can Lily find a magical unicorn in time?

THE LITTLEST PIRATE

SHERRYL CLARK

Nicholas Nosh is the littlest pirate in the world. He's not allowed to go to sea. 'You're too small,' said his dad. But when the fierce pirate Captain Red Beard kidnaps his family, Nicholas sets sail to rescue them!

Nobody is better at being bad than Buster Reed – he flicks paint, says rude words to girls, sticks chewing gum under the seats and wears the same socks for weeks at a time. Naturally no one wants to know him. But Buster has a secret – he would like a friend to play with. How will he ever manage to find one?

Tom was given a gorilla suit for his birthday. He loved it and wore it everywhere. When mum and dad took him to the zoo he wouldn't wear his ordinary clothes. But isn't it asking for trouble to go to the zoo dressed as a gorilla?

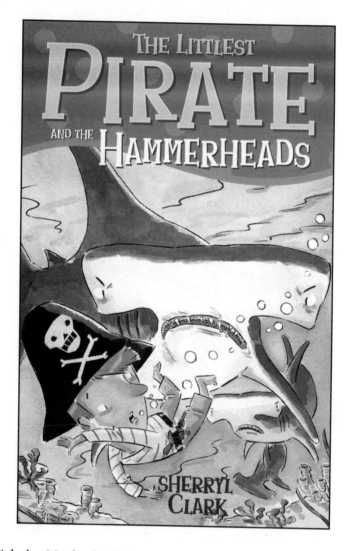

Nicholas Nosh, the littlest pirate in the world, has to rescue his family's treasure which has been stolen by Captain Hammerhead. But how can he outwit the sharks that are guarding Captain Hammerhead's ship?

When Anna Slept Over

Jane Godwin

Josie is Anna's best friend. Anna has played at Josie's house, she's even stayed for dinner, but she has never slept over. Until now…

Crystal longs to be a mermaid.
Her mother makes her a flashing silver tail. But it isn't like
being a proper mermaid. Then one night Crystal wears her
tail to bed...